Oliver Moon's Summer Howliday

Sue Mongredien

Illustrated by

Jan McCafferty

USBORNE

For Archie Ryder, with lots of love

First published in 2006 by Usborne Publishing Ltd., Usborne House, 83-85 Saffron Hill, London EC1N 8RT, England. www.usborne.com

Text copyright © Sue Mongredien, 2006
Illustration copyright © Usborne Publishing Ltd., 2006

A CIP catalogue record for this book is available from the British Library.

UK ISBN 9780746077924 First published in America in 2010 AE.
American ISBN 9780794527594

FMAMJJASOND/10 94163

Printed in Yeovil, Somerset, UK.

Contents

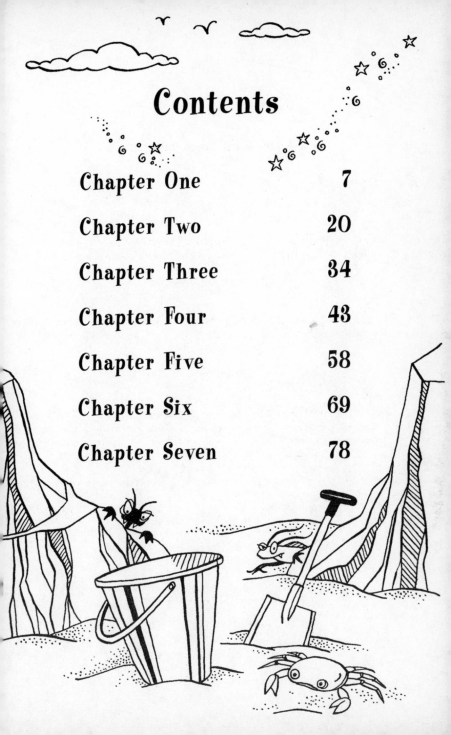

Chapter One

Oliver Moon folded his swim trunks and put them on top of the pile of clothes on his bed. There! That was everything he needed. He was *really* looking forward to going on vacation. He couldn't wait!

Oliver waved his wand over the suitcase that was on the floor nearby.

"Click, clock, clack… Clothes be packed!" he chanted.

He grinned as his suitcase promptly opened up, and his clothes flew inside, arranging themselves neatly. Being a wizard came in very handy sometimes!

Mrs. Moon, Oliver's mom, came into
the bedroom just then, followed by the
Witch Baby, Oliver's sister, who was
wearing a shiny silver bucket on
her head. "Vacation *now*!"
the Witch Baby was
saying excitedly,
trying to dig up
Oliver's carpet
with her new
silver spade.
"Vacation now?"

Mrs. Moon smiled. "Nearly," she said.
"Oh good, Oliver, you're all packed. I'll
send your case off to the beach house,
with the rest of our things." She waved
her wand over Oliver's case, and a swirl
of purple sparkles drifted across it as she

began chanting the address: "Mildew Cottage, Forest Lane, Little...*atchoo*!" She sneezed suddenly and blew her nose with a large black handkerchief.

Before she could say another word, Oliver's suitcase had vanished in a bright purple flash.

"No, wait, come back!" Mrs. Moon shouted in alarm, stuffing her handkerchief back in her cloak pocket. "I hadn't finished!"

Oliver stared at the spot on the floor where his case had been. His suitcase, with all his favorite clothes, new swim trunks, new Frisbee and his very best cool-wizard sunglasses! "But…where's my stuff gone?" he asked.

"Gone!" sang the Witch Baby, tripping over her spade and giggling. "Gone, gone, gone."

Mrs. Moon looked sheepish. "I'm not sure," she confessed. "Hopefully to the right place. I've been sending odds and ends to Little Spelling-on-Sea all morning. With a bit of luck, the wand

will know where to send your case, too."
She crossed her fingers quickly.

A shout came up from Mr. Moon, who
was downstairs. "Let's go!"

"We'd better not keep your dad
waiting," Mrs. Moon said, picking up the
Witch Baby and heading for the door.
"Come on, Oliver. Time to fly!"

Little Spelling-on-Sea was about an hour's
broomstick ride away from the Moons'
home in Cacklewick. It was a small village,
nestled in the coastline, with a golden,
sandy beach, and dark, spooky forests.

"It's this one, I think!" Mr. Moon
called, pointing his broomstick down in
the direction of a large garden just near
the beach.

Oliver steered his broomstick toward
his parents and landed on the grass
moments later.

Mrs. Moon unstrapped the Witch Baby
from her baby seat. "Very nice," she said
approvingly, looking around.

Oliver agreed. There was a fine crop of nettles and poison ivy on one side of the lawn, and a sour-plum tree on the other, with a rope swing hanging from one of its branches. There was an outside cauldron that had been set up for barbecues, and a picnic bench too.

His sister was already toddling eagerly toward the large sludge-filled pond, where a family of friendly looking toads was croaking a welcome. "Nice toads!" she beamed, patting them each on the head.

At the far end of the garden was a dense pine forest from which strange animal calls could be heard.

"It's really cool here!" Oliver said with a grin. "Can we look around the cottage, Dad?"

Mr. Moon held out his hand and a bunch of keys appeared in it, with a clinking sound. "Definitely," he replied. "And then we'd better think about catching something for supper. I might even crank up that outdoor cauldron."

"Good idea," said Mrs. Moon happily.

"Me swim now?" the Witch Baby asked, dabbling a toe in the pond.

Mrs. Moon quickly pointed her wand at the pond and a large wire mesh appeared over it, before the Witch Baby could go any deeper. "We'll swim in the sea later, pumpkin," she promised. "But let's go and explore our vacation cottage now." She scooped up the Witch Baby and began walking toward the back door. "I love this place already! I do hope we see the ghost while we're here."

"Ghost?" Oliver echoed, turning to her in interest.

Mrs. Moon nodded. "Didn't I say? The cottage is haunted, apparently. That's what it said in the brochure, anyway."

"Cool!" Oliver grinned. He couldn't help wondering what the ghost looked like. Perhaps it would be the ghost of an old wizard or witch, a really ancient, spooky one. Or maybe it would be a ghost *boy* that Oliver could play with!

He ran ahead to the cottage and
peered in through the grimy windows.
Imagine how jealous Jake, his best friend
back home in Cacklewick, would be if
Oliver sent him a postcard saying he'd
met a real ghost on his vacation!

Chapter
Two

Mr. Moon unlocked the back door and
the whole family went inside. They
found themselves in a small, smelly
kitchen, with a couple of rats skittering
across the draining board, and an
impressive collection of cockroaches
on the walls, spelling WELCOME in
large letters.

"Oh, lovely," Mrs. Moon cooed. "Very homely!"

Next to the kitchen, there was a living room with mold-patterned curtains and a strong stench of mildew and hogweed. A door led through to a dining room with dead snakes tastefully arranged on the mantelpiece. Then Oliver spotted the twisty staircase that led up to the bedrooms, and they all rushed upstairs.

The first bedroom
was small, with a cot
by the window, and
a monster-mobile
dangling above it.
"Mine!" squeaked the
Witch Baby at once, rattling
the bars of the cot with great excitement.

Next there was a medium-sized
bedroom for Oliver, with a sea view, and
posters of fierce-looking trolls on the
walls. And last was the biggest bedroom
of all, with a moldy double bed, and a
huge pile of luggage on the floor.

"Oh good, it's arrived," Mrs. Moon
said, making a beeline for the cases.
"Here are the baby things, and here are
the bathroom things…"

"Is my stuff there?" Oliver asked hopefully.

"Oliver's case – show yourself!" Mrs. Moon chanted, twirling her wand.

There was a dead silence. Nothing moved. "Oh dear," said Mr. Moon. "I wonder where that one's got to?"

"I sneezed right in the middle of the Transporta spell," Mrs. Moon told him, and bit her lip. "Is there a village called Little Sneezing, I wonder?"

"I've got a feeling there is," Mr. Moon replied. "A boggy, swampy kind of place, I seem to remember." He fixed a bright smile on his face at the sight of Oliver's doleful expression. "Not to worry, Oliver. We'll find your things. You can borrow some of my pajamas for tonight."

"Thanks," said Oliver, but he couldn't help feeling a pang of gloom as he thought about his Frisbee and trunks.

He hated the idea of them being down at the bottom of a swamp. Anything could have eaten them by now!

"Maybe we could cast a Bring-back spell," Mrs. Moon wondered. "*Atchoo!* How does it go again?"

"I'll do it," Oliver said quickly, as his mom reached for her handkerchief and blew her nose again. He didn't want another sneeze to send his case somewhere else! He waved his wand and chanted, "Vacation place, bring-back case!"

Nothing happened for a moment, and then a deafening crash was heard in Oliver's bedroom. He raced in there to find his suitcase, dripping wet and covered with pondweed, on the floor.

Oliver brushed off the weed, and
saw that the zip had split on one side
of the case.

He unzipped the rest of it, and pushed
the lid back to check everything was still
there. His trunks felt a bit soggy, but

they'd dry off soon enough. A swamp-eel was coiled up inside his Frisbee, but that was all right.

"And I'll have those back, thank you very much," Oliver said, whipping his funky sunglasses off a large brown toad.

Oliver wiped his sunglasses clean on his T-shirt and perched them on top of his head, feeling much happier. Yesss!

He had everything he needed for a fantastic summer vacation… Now all he had to do was find the ghost!

"Cheers!" said Mr. Moon, raising his glass of black beetlebeer a few hours later. It was early evening, and the family had spent the afternoon down on the beach, swimming in the sea and building a massive sandcastle together. Now they were all back at the cottage, munching the barbecued sea slugs that Oliver and his dad had caught for supper.

"Cheers," Mrs. Moon echoed, lifting her starfish wine and clinking it with her husband's glass.

"Cheers," Oliver added, raising his cup of pond water.

"Cheese," echoed the Witch Baby, hoisting up the large, pink crab she'd found on the beach. "Smelly cheese!"

Oliver couldn't stop smiling. It was warm enough for them all to be eating outside at the picnic table, and the sun was just dipping below the tops of the forest trees. The sea slugs were juicy and fresh, and his nose tingled where it had caught the sun.

"Bliss," Oliver's mom sighed. "Now I really feel like we're on vacation."

Mr. Moon drained his beer and let out a loud belch that rattled the cottage windows. "Yes, we're definitely going to have a good week here," he proclaimed. "I can feel it in my—"

HOWWWWWWLLLLL!

Mr. Moon broke off as a ferocious howling started up from the forest behind them. The sun was blood-red now as it sank lower through the trees.

"What was that?" Oliver asked, staring into the forest. The howling died away and a deathly silence fell. He could feel goosebumps prickling all the way down his back, and he shivered as a sudden breeze blew up.

"Doggy!" said the Witch Baby brightly, straining in her high chair to see. "Where doggy?"

Mrs. Moon had turned pale. She shook her head slowly. "No, darling, that wasn't a doggy," she said nervously. "I think…"

HOWWWLLLLLLL!

Oliver's parents exchanged glances, and Mr. Moon swallowed. "I think that was a werewolf," he said.

Chapter
Three

"A werewolf?" echoed Oliver, his eyes wide. "But there isn't a full moon tonight. I thought—"

"Some werewolves don't need a full moon to transform," Mr. Moon said and grimaced. "Some change every evening as soon as night falls."

"I knew it was too good to be true."

Mrs. Moon sighed, looking glum. "No wonder this cottage was so cheap to rent!"

"I hope we get to see a werewolf while we're here!" Oliver said, eagerly. "That would be amazing!"

Mr. Moon gave a shudder. "No, it wouldn't," he said. "It'd eat us alive! It'd tear us limb from limb and gobble up our brains!" He glanced over at the Witch Baby. "It'd chomp up your sister in one single mouthful."

"Would it really?" Oliver asked. His mouth hung open. "Wow."

Mrs. Moon gave her husband a warning look. "We'll be fine, as long as we stay out of the forest," she said, turning back to Oliver and the Witch

Baby. "So no wandering off on your own, you two, especially after dark. Understand?"

"Not wander," said the Witch Baby. Her bottom lip trembled and a tear splashed down her cheek. "Not chomp me!"

"Now look what you've done!" Mrs. Moon said reproachfully to Mr. Moon. She kissed the Witch Baby's little nose.

"Nobody's going to chomp you up, darling. Daddy's only being silly."

HOWWWWWLLLLLL!

"Sounds like there's more than one of them out there," Mr. Moon said. "They'll be keeping us awake all night, you wait."

Mrs. Moon nodded. "When I was a little witch, there was a pack of the wretched creatures near our house," she said. "The racket they used to make was quite shocking! Never a thought for anyone else. So selfish!"

HOWWWWWLLLLLLL!

"I'll have to magic up some earplugs for us all," Mr. Moon said crossly, spearing his last sea slug with his fork. "Otherwise we'll *never* get to sleep tonight."

Oliver stared into the darkness of the

forest, not listening to his parents anymore. As far as he was concerned, werewolves were really, *really* cool. In fact, he hoped he could meet the ghost *and* a werewolf while he was in Little Spelling-on-Sea! Wouldn't that be *amazing*?

It was very exciting to lie in bed and fall asleep to the howls of the werewolves that night. Oliver slept well and bounced out of bed early the next morning. He was looking forward to getting back to the beach and trying out his new Frisbee today. It was a special star-shaped one that he'd spotted in the Wizards' Toy Emporium and had saved up for weeks to buy.

Mrs. Moon was sneezing into the slug oatmeal at the kitchen stove when Oliver

went in. She looked bleary-eyed and
bad-tempered, and was muttering
about no sleep.

"Wasn't your bed very comfortable?"
Oliver asked sympathetically.

"The bed was fine." Mrs. Moon snorted.
"It was those awful werewolves howling

all night in the forest that kept me awake. Your dad, too. He's trying to catch up on his sleep now."

"HOWWWLLLL!" screeched the Witch Baby, waving her spoon around. Oliver noticed that she still had her crab with her, and seemed to have made it a little sleeping bag out of one of her purple socks.

"Exactly," Mrs. Moon said through gritted teeth, rubbing her temples.

Oliver decided he would take his batwing toast outside, to eat at the picnic table in the garden. It was always wise to

give his mom a wide berth when she was
in a grumpy mood. When he opened the
back door, though, he saw that the
garden was a complete mess. Litter blew
about the lawn, and the garbage cans
were lying on their sides.

"Oh, no!" his mom exclaimed, when she came outside. "Those stupid werewolves must have knocked over the garbage cans! Honestly! I've a good mind to pack up and go straight back home this morning!"

"Don't do that," Oliver said hurriedly. "Look, I'll clean up. It won't take long."

His mom shut the back door, and Oliver got to work. It was only a small bit of litter, after all, he thought. And the last thing he wanted to do was go home early. Their vacation had only just begun – and there was no way Oliver wanted to leave Little Spelling-on-Sea without seeing the werewolves and ghost!

Chapter
Four

Once Mr. Moon was up and everyone was dressed, Mrs. Moon consulted the barometer on the kitchen wall.

"A showery morning," it announced in a sing-song voice, "followed by a sunny afternoon."

Oliver looked out of the window, where it was just starting to drizzle.

"Looks like the beach is off for a while," his dad said thoughtfully. "How about a stroll into the village? We could do with picking up a few odds and ends. And I think there's a good Monster Museum we could visit."

Oliver nodded, liking the sound of the Monster Museum.

"Whoopee!" his sister cheered, throwing the crab up in the air and catching it in her sundress.

"Good idea," his mom said, yawning. "I'll see if I can pick up the ingredients for a sleep potion while we're there."

Little Spelling-on-Sea was a small village with a bustling market, a village green, a Magic Supplies shop and the Monster Museum, as well as a couple of cafés.

In the market, Mrs. Moon bought her potion ingredients and a new green lipstick. Mr. Moon picked up a book he'd been wanting to read and some bait for his fishing rod. The Witch Baby chose some bat-patterned swim armbands that she insisted on blowing up and wearing as soon as they'd been paid for, and Oliver bought a pair of sand-skis and some postcards.

It was still raining, so they headed into the Monster Museum next. Spooky music was playing as they wandered around the scary waxwork models of vampires, ghouls, trolls and other monsters. Oliver stopped in front of the werewolf model and stared at it, feeling breathless with excitement.

WEREWOLF
LYCANTHROPUS

Werewolf, **lycanthropus**, the sign next to it read.

A werewolf is a person who changes into a wolf, either by magic, or under a curse, at nighttime. A werewolf grows fur all over its body, its eyes glow red, and it walks on all fours. Werewolves hunt for prey in forests by the light of the moon, and have a distinctive howl. They dislike silver and are afraid of water. They also...

"HOOWWWLLLLL!"

Oliver almost jumped out of his skin at the noise right behind him. He turned around in fright...only to see his dad roaring with laughter. "Gotcha!" his dad guffawed. "You should have seen the look on your face, Oliver!"

"Ssshhhh!" hissed one of the museum

attendants, a wrinkled old hag who
looked about two thousand years old.

"Da-ad!" Oliver groaned.

Mr. Moon clapped him on the shoulder. "Come on, son, let's go to the beach now," he said. "The sun's out, and your sister's desperate to find another crab. She just lost hers somewhere in the sea-serpent tank."

Oliver gave the werewolf a last look, and followed his dad. Now that he'd seen how awesome the model werewolf was, he was keener than ever to see the real thing.

Once on the beach, Oliver wasted no time in trying out his new Frisbee. It was a Sparkle-Skimma model, which left drifts of electric-blue sparkles in its wake and made a high-pitched shrieking noise as it whizzed through the air. It was easy to

catch, too, and Oliver and his dad spent a very pleasant half-hour throwing it back and forth to each other, while Mrs. Moon helped the Witch Baby build a sand palace for the new crab she'd found.

After a picnic lunch of centipede sandwiches and worm juice, Oliver was keen to play Frisbee again, but his dad was firmly settled in a beach chaise with his new book, and his mom had dozed off under her pointy hat. The Witch Baby couldn't throw or catch very well yet, and besides, she was busily eating some burrow-beetles she'd just discovered in her sand palace.

Oliver spun his Frisbee around on his finger and looked up and down the beach, wondering what to do next.

"I'll have a game with you, if you want," a voice said from behind him, and a boy of around Oliver's age strode up. He had brown curly hair, bushy eyebrows, and a wide smile. "I'm Wilf," he said. "What's your name?"

"Oliver," Oliver told him, smiling back. "Do you live round here, or are you on vacation?" he asked, pacing backward and throwing the Frisbee to Wilf.

"I'm a local," Wilf said, jumping up to catch it. "Nice," he said approvingly, looking at the Frisbee more closely. "Is it a Sparkle-Skimma? I've always wanted one of those. They are *sooo* cool."

Wilf threw it back to Oliver, who sent
it whizzing straight back again. Wilf ran
to grab it, but the wind chose that very
moment to start up, and blew the Frisbee
straight into the sea.

Oliver waited for Wilf to wade in and fetch it but, to his surprise, Wilf stood staring at the waves with a nervous expression on his face. "Um… Could you get it?" he called to Oliver. "I don't like the sea."

Oliver raised his eyebrows. "You don't like the sea?" he echoed in surprise.

Wilf shook his head, stepping back as a wave crept up the beach toward him. Oliver shrugged and went to get his Frisbee. He *loved* the sea. He couldn't understand why anyone wouldn't!

Oliver and Wilf played Frisbee for ages, and then Oliver remembered his new sand-skis. He and Wilf took them up to the highest sand dune and used one each to whiz down it, as if they were on skateboards. It was so much fun!

Oliver was enjoying himself so much that he lost track of the time. It was only when Wilf gasped and said he had to go home that Oliver realized the sun was starting to go down.

"One last time?" Oliver said hopefully, holding his sand-ski.

Wilf shook his head. "Gotta dash," he replied, dropping the other sand-ski

and rushing up the sand dune away from Oliver. "Bye! See you again!"

"Bye!" Oliver called after him. He was glad to have made a friend so quickly. He gazed out to sea, feeling a surge of happiness rush through him. Lunch on the beach…a new friend…playing Frisbee all afternoon… Everything was turning out perfectly!

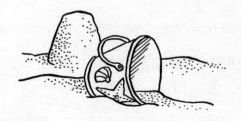

Chapter Five

The next few days passed very enjoyably.
The Moon family got up late every
morning, had breakfast
in the garden with
the friendly toads,
then packed up
a picnic lunch to
take to the beach.

Oliver and Wilf had a lot of fun together each day, playing Frisbee and beach volleyball, and whizzing down the sand dunes on Oliver's new skis. Oliver couldn't help wondering if Wilf's parents were a bit strict, though. Wilf always rushed home as soon as the sun started going down, as if he was worried they'd punish him if he came home late.

On the fourth day of the vacation, Oliver got to meet Wilf's parents when they came to join the Moons for lunch on the beach. And actually, they weren't strict at all – they were lovely! Wilf's dad, Wayne, had quite the hairiest back Oliver had ever seen, but was very nice and friendly. Wilf's mom, Wendy, had long brown hair and very white teeth, and smiled a lot.

"You must all come round to us one evening," Mrs. Moon said warmly, waving her wand over the Thermos flask to pour everyone toadstool tea. "We've got a lovely outdoor cauldron for barbecues…"

"…And we could sink a few beetlebeers together," Mr. Moon added with a grin.

Wayne and Wendy looked at each other. "Um… We're quite busy in the evenings," Wayne said apologetically. "We've got a lot going on at the moment."

"Oh," said Mrs. Moon, waiting for him to explain. He didn't.

"Thanks for asking us," Wendy said, tucking her hair behind her ears. "It's just…. Oh! Oh!"

She jumped up suddenly as if something had burned her, and Oliver looked around to see what it was.

"Peekaboo!" the Witch Baby chortled, from where she was hiding under her silver bucket. She lifted it off her head and grinned toothily at everyone. "Peekaboo!"

"Peekaboo, darling!" Mrs. Moon cooed back at her.

"Everything all right?" Mr. Moon asked, looking curiously at Wendy.

"Yes, of course," Wendy replied, sitting a little further away from the Witch Baby. "Ahhh...what a...what a sweetheart. She just made me jump, that's all."

The Witch Baby was shuffling toward Wilf now, with the bucket on her head once more. "Peekaboo!" she was shouting in a muffled voice.

Wilf edged away from her, as if he was pretending to be scared. "Who is this strange creature?" he said jokily, backing off.

The Witch Baby yanked the bucket off her head and grinned broadly. "Me," she announced, jabbing herself in the chest. "Me strange!"

"You're right about that one," Oliver laughed, passing around the squashed fly cookies. Wayne took a cookie from the plate and Oliver suddenly noticed just how hairy his hands were, as well as his back. Even his palms were hairy!

In fact, Oliver thought, trying not to
stare, Wayne was easily the hairiest
person he'd ever seen. Hair sprouted out
of his nostrils and ears, and all over his
belly, almost as if he were a...

"Want to play a game of Frisbee?"
Wilf said just then, and Oliver jumped,
realizing that he was gawping.

"Yeah," Oliver said, getting to his feet.
"Let's go!"

That night, Oliver started writing a
postcard to his best friend at home.

Dear Jake,

*Having a MAGIC time at Little Spelling.
Our cottage is haunted (haven't seen any ghosts
yet but fingers crossed I will soon) AND there
are werewolves in the forest nearby. We hear
them howling every night; it's dead exciting,
although Mom and Dad just moan about them
making a racket and knocking the garbage cans
over all the time. Who cares about a bit of noise
and litter, though? Not me – I am dying to see
one of them!*

*Have met this boy Wilf who is loads of
fun, but*

Oliver stopped writing. He couldn't
quite put his finger on what he thought
about Wilf. There was definitely

something a bit strange about him and his family. Wayne's hairiness. The way Wendy had seemed so afraid of the Witch Baby when she'd had the silver bucket on her head. And fancy Wilf not liking the sea! It was almost as if he was scared of the water or something!

HOWWWWLLLLLLL!

Oliver jumped as the howling started up outside, and then his mouth fell open in shock as a crazy thought hit him. Hadn't it said in the Monster Museum that werewolves were afraid of silver and water? But surely Wilf and his family couldn't possibly be werewolves… could they?

Chapter Six

"Oliver! Dinner's ready!"

His mind whirling, Oliver rushed downstairs and out to the garden, where his dad had just taken a large squid off the barbecue and was serving up its slimy tentacles onto plates.

HOWWWWWLLLLLL!

There they were again. *Surely the*

werewolves couldn't really be Wilf and his family? Oliver thought. He must have had too much sun to imagine such a thing!

"Honestly, I wish they'd give it a rest for one night," Mrs. Moon snapped irritably, as a second werewolf started howling, then a third. "That noise does havoc on my nerves."

"Why are you so against werewolves, anyway?" Oliver asked with interest. "What have they ever done to you?"

At Oliver's question, the howling in the forest stopped immediately. It was almost as if the werewolves were listening to hear Mrs. Moon's answer.

"Oh, they're a dangerous lot," Mrs. Moon said darkly.

"Untrustworthy," Mr. Moon agreed, squirting termite-o ketchup on his plate. "Far inferior to witches and wizards."

"They can't even do magic," Mrs. Moon sniffed.

"Hairy scary," the Witch Baby put in with a knowing air.

"Have you ever met one, though?" Oliver asked. "There might be some

really nice werewolves for all you know —
just like there are plenty of dangerous,
untrustworthy wizards and witches."

"Met one? Of course not!" Mrs. Moon
said.

"Why would we want to do a thing like
that?" Mr. Moon shuddered. "Horrible
beasts."

"Inconsiderate, as well as noisy," Mrs.
Moon said, squishing a squid's eye onto
the end of her fork and biting it in half.

"The way they keep knocking over the garbage cans. Trying to get our leftovers, no doubt. Huh!"

Oliver's mind was racing, trying to make sense of his suspicions about Wilf. He couldn't help glancing toward the forest, where it was still unusually quiet.

If Wilf and his family really *were* the werewolves, then he hoped that they weren't listening to what the Moons were saying about them.

"Well, I think werewolves are great," he said loudly, just in case they could hear. "My teacher at school says they've got excellent tracking skills and a brilliant sense of smell."

"Pah! I'd rather have a magic wand and a few spells up my sleeve any day," Mr. Moon said firmly.

"Wand," the Witch Baby agreed. She stretched out a hand for Mrs. Moon's wand that had been left on the picnic table. "Wand!"

"I don't think you should be..." Oliver started saying as his sister banged it noisily on the tray of her high chair.

"Careful, sweetie," Mrs. Moon said, sipping her drink, her eyes still on the forest.

"Wandy wand," the Witch Baby went on singing. "Wandy wandy w—"

Oliver stared at the high chair where his sister had been sitting only seconds before and rubbed his eyes.

"And another thing," Oliver's mom began saying, but Oliver interrupted her.

"Mom! Dad!" he shouted, pointing at the empty high chair. "Look! The Witch Baby's vanished!"

Chapter
Seven

Mrs. Moon gave a scream.

Mr. Moon gave a yell.

Then there came a distant wail.

"Mommy!"

And a howl. **HOWWWLLLLLL!**

"It sounds as if she's in the forest!"
gulped Mrs. Moon. "My baby – all alone,
with those bloodthirsty werewolves!"

Oliver, his mom and dad all rushed
down the garden to the forest at once.
"I'll try a Summoning spell," Mr. Moon
panted, waving his wand.
"By the power of
night and this
forest shady,
I summon the
sweetest green-
haired baby! Oh,
drat! My wand's
got sand in it,
it won't work!"
"And I've left *my* wand in my room,"
Oliver groaned as they reached the
edge of the forest. His mom's wand
had disappeared with the Witch
Baby, so they didn't have that, either.

Magic wasn't going to help them now! "We'll just have to find her ourselves."

"Where are you? Where are you, pumpkin?" Mrs. Moon bellowed.

There was only another wail in reply. "Want…my…mommy!"

"We're coming! We'll find you!" Mrs. Moon cried in anguish.

The forest seemed to be growing darker by the minute as they followed one path, and then another. Before long, Oliver felt completely lost. It seemed as if they were going round in circles! The moon was hidden behind a cloud, and the light was very dim under the rustling branches. Owls hooted. A squabblehawk screeched. And still the werewolves went on howling.

Then Oliver had an idea. It had to be worth a try. He took a deep breath.

"Wilf!" he shouted at the top of his voice. "Wilf, if you're there, can you help find my sister?"

"What are you talking about?" his dad snapped, puffing and panting behind him. "This is no time to be messing about, Oliver!"

But just then, the moon slid out from behind the clouds, lighting the forest with silver. And as it did so, Oliver and his family could see that further along the path, stood a red-eyed werewolf... holding the Witch Baby!

"Don't eat her!" screamed Mrs. Moon.
"Please! Don't hurt her!"

The werewolf stared at them. "Eat her?
Hurt her?" it said. "Of course I won't!
I'm a vegetarian, you know!" He fixed

Mrs. Moon with a severe look. "Just because some werewolves eat people, it doesn't mean we all do."

"Wilfy-wolf!" the Witch Baby giggled, stroking his furry face. "Nice wolf."

Mrs. Moon stopped dead, and Oliver and Mr. Moon almost cannoned into her. "Wilf!" Oliver cried in relief. "It *is* you!" He pushed past his parents, who seemed rooted to the spot in shock. "You found her!"

Wilf handed the Witch Baby over to Oliver as he drew nearer. Wilf was furry all over, with pointy ears, a lolling, red tongue and sharp, white teeth.

"You guessed my secret then," he said, a strange expression on his face. "So you probably don't want to be friends with me now, right?"

Oliver started in surprise. "Of course I do!" he replied.

His mom and dad had crept closer, nervous expressions on their faces. Oliver passed the Witch Baby to his mom, but she seemed too shocked to be able to speak.

"I think werewolves are awesome," Oliver went on. He grinned. "Especially if you can show us how to get out of this forest and back home again."

Wilf smiled. "No problem," he said. "This way!"

Wilf led the Moons back to their garden

— where a curious, shimmering dog was busily sniffing around the upturned garbage cans.

At the sound of their footsteps, the dog turned toward them, a guilty expression on its face...and promptly vanished into thin air!

"A ghost *dog*!" Oliver whistled. "So *that's* who's been knocking over the garbage cans every night – not the werewolves!"

Mr. and Mrs. Moon seemed to have recovered from the shock of seeing Wilf as a werewolf, and were now looking extremely shamefaced. Mrs. Moon gave an embarrassed cough. "Sorry, Wilf," she said. "We got werewolves all wrong." She cuddled the Witch Baby. "Your tracking skills were a lot more useful than our magic tonight," she added sheepishly.

Wilf shrugged, then gave a cheeky grin. "Hey, now that you've all seen me in my hairy glory, maybe I could come to one of your barbecues sometime…that's if I'm still invited?" he asked.

"Of course you're invited!" Mr. Moon
cried.

"Bring the whole hairy family!" Mrs.
Moon added. "The more the merrier!"

*

On the last evening of the vacation, there was a very special get-together at Mildew Cottage. Mr. and Mrs. Moon made a delicious vegetarian broth in the outdoor cauldron for their new friends, Wilf, Wayne and Wendy, and there was music and dancing in the garden all night long. Wilf taught Oliver and the Witch Baby how to howl at the moon. Mr. and Mrs. Moon put on a magic show for everyone, including a magical fireworks display. And then Wayne and Wendy taught everyone how to dance the Hairy Shuffle.

"Cheers to new friends!" Mr. Moon said, brandishing his beer in the air.

"Cheers!" everyone replied.

"And cheers to summer holidays," Oliver grinned. "Or should that be summer *howl*idays?"

"HOOWWWWLLLLL!" the Witch Baby bellowed. And everyone laughed.

The End

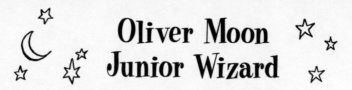

Oliver Moon
Junior Wizard

Collect all of Oliver Moon's magical adventures!

Oliver Moon's Fangtastic Sleepover
Will Oliver survive a school sleepover in the haunted house museum?

Oliver Moon and the Broomstick Battle
Can Oliver beat Bully to win the Junior Wizards' Obstacle Race?

Happy Birthday, Oliver Moon
Will Oliver's birthday party be ruined when his invitations go astray?

Oliver Moon and the Spider Spell
Oliver's Grow-bigger spell lands the Witch Baby's pet in huge trouble.

Oliver Moon and the Troll Trouble
Can Oliver save the show as the scary, stinky troll in the school play?

Oliver Moon and the Monster Mystery
Strange things start to happen when Oliver wins a monster raffle prize...

Don't miss Oliver's fab website,
where you can find lots of fun, free stuff.
Log on now...

www.olivermoon.com